Things I Wish I'd Said

for Viv

with love

Contents

Foreword

Medusa - 5

Anne Boleyn - 8

Mary Boleyn - 12

Helen of Troy - 15

Anne Hathaway - 17

Pandora - 20

Lady Macbeth - 22

Wendy - 24

Mrs Claus - 26

Foreword

This anthology is a collection of monologues written from the perspectives of unheard women throughout history, literature and mythology. Although these monologues are based on existing characters or indeed people, I have used a liberal amount of creative licence in expressing what I imagine their thoughts to be.

There are, of course, many more stories to be told.

Medusa

Medusa is arguably the most famous character from Greek mythology, known for her hair of snakes, and gaze that would turn you to stone. There are several versions of the tale of Medusa, all of which culminate in her death at the hands of Perseus. Some stories describe her as a monster from birth, the only mortal of one of three Gorgon sisters; others depict her as being an attractive woman turned into a monster by Athena after being raped by Poseidon in Athena's temple.

I was beautiful once. Call me vain if you like, but don't pretend it isn't what every woman seeks to be, because the pitiable truth is that is how our value is determined.

To Athena, I had devoted my life, and yet, when Poseidon came, when he stole my joy, my dignity and my pride, she declared I had defiled her temple and decided to curse me further.

Why was it I that was punished for the sin that another committed against me?

I still recall how I scrambled up from my crumpled position on the ground, tripping over the torn fabric of my dress with my heart hammering in my chest in response to the soft hiss in my ear. It was then that fresh tears began to join the recently dried ones on my cheeks, and my whole body trembled as I saw how my long flowing curls had congealed into a dark, writhing mass that spat and hissed as I turned my head.

In a frenzied attempt to escape my own repulsive form, I had bolted from the temple, only to discover the other, more chilling alteration in myself: my stony gaze.

I still see her eyes, those of the sweet and innocent woman who became my first victim: soft, honey-brown and pleading.

I had stood there, my own eyes wide in horror as this woman remained motionless, while a greyish colouring crept up her body, taking over her features. As I raced through the streets, many had followed her in their fate.

Inwardly I swear I am no monster, outwardly perhaps, but not inwardly. So I fled. I had seen what I was capable of, and I would not, could not allow myself to cause any more harm.

Now I inhabit this desolate cavern scattered with the statues of those who ventured to eliminate me.

They began to arrive shortly after myself, evidently hearing of the trail of destruction I had left in my wake.

I took no pleasure in ending these men, but you see, it was kill or be killed, and it was so easy, too easy, just one look.

That was when I still had hope, faith that this could not be my forever and that someday I would be freed from this lonely hell.

Now I recognise that no one will save a monster, but people can always be relied upon to try to destroy what they perceive to be wrong. It is only a matter of time.

So, I await him now, Perseus, I know he's coming.

Soon he will boast of his courage in putting down the bestial Medusa. Let him.

Only you will know the truth: I simply gave up, for there are few who could stand to exist as I have.

Soon it will be over. Maybe I will be beautiful again.

Anne Boleyn

Anne Boleyn was the second wife of Henry VIII. She was beheaded for high treason after having been accused of adultery and plotting against the King.

There is a significant chance that she was innocent and her only 'crime' being to have not provided the King with a son.

They say there is no rest for the wicked, but I can tell you that it is those judged by others to be wicked, but with no true wickedness in their heart, who may not rest.

Sleep evades me and tomorrow I shall die.

They will lead me to the scaffold on Tower Green; I feel I can hear the faint hammering of its assembly now, though I know this to be a phantom for it is near midnight.

I shall slowly ascend the steps. I shall not stumble.

I shall stand central to the scaffold, and I shall give my last address to the crowd. My voice will not falter. As I sit here now, I ponder what I shall say.

I shall not protest my innocence for those closest to me know the truth, and it is too late now to alter the minds of the masses. Besides, what would be the point? The only man who can change my fate is Henry himself. For a while I believed he may offer an eleventh-hour reprieve, but I know now this will not be the case. Perhaps he has deluded himself into believing his fabricated charges in order to remove any sense of guilt.

He will not be there tomorrow as we both know that seeing the accusation in these dark eyes that once displayed such warmth, would not allow him to continue in his guiltless fantasy.

But you see, I need him to feel shame, to recognise his wrongdoing because, despite his claims, deep down he knows that heaven itself could not have moved me to betray him. Clearly, this loyalty was far from reciprocated and that has caused me another kind of grief.

So, although I will not see him myself, as his cowardice prevents him from facing me, he will be given an account of how I faced my end.

My final words will for that reason be full of praise for the King and those sweet words will haunt him for far longer than any reproachful speech because he will know that they hold no truth.

That is my selfish reason for delivering an address that does not contain a single word that I actually believe.

My ulterior motive is my daughter. I must ensure that she does not pay the consequences of my actions, for although her age should mean that she can only be considered blameless, I saw how Henry treated Mary after he divorced her mother. Elizabeth must not suffer that same fate.

The few that remain loyal to me have assured me that they will strive to protect her and that one day, when she is older, she will hear my truth.

Henry desires a son and heir, but I know Elizabeth will be as capable as any man and, if she were ever to reach the throne, would prove to be a greater ruler than he.

I must live through her now, and so I will hold onto my dignity to the last.

He will not see me crumble.

Once I have spoken, my ladies will help me to remove my cape and jewels. My hands will not tremble.

I shall thank them for their service. I shall shed no tears.

To the swordsman I shall give a sack of coins as his payment and offer him my forgiveness. It is not he who ends my life, not really.

My eyes will not search for the sword which is to commit me to my grave.

I shall kneel.

My face will not betray my fear.

Then there will be the singing of a blade, darkness, and finally I shall sleep.

Mary Boleyn

Mary Boleyn, sister of Anne, was Henry VIII's mistress before he turned his attention to Anne. She was also rumoured to have been the mistress of Francis I of France, but there is very little evidence to support this. She was married to William Carey during the course of her affair with the King, and it is unknown whether the two children born during this period were fathered by her husband or Henry VIII. Her second husband, William Stafford, was of a lower rank than her, and she married him in secret, resulting in her being banished from Court by the now Queen Anne and the King. It is likely that she never saw Anne again.

If you know me at all, then you will know me as the other Boleyn girl, but I would instead suggest you think of me as the Boleyn who survived.

We were pitted against each other since we were children, Anne and I. It suited our family as, by competing against each other, we pushed ourselves further. They never cared who succeeded as long as it was one of us.

I learnt the truth of that too late, when I returned to Court after the birth of my second child to find the King, the father of my children, wrapped around the little finger of my sister.

My feelings were irrelevant to my family. As far as they were concerned, as long as one of us was in favour, then the family would profit and that was all that mattered.

I had been cast aside like a toy that was no longer interesting.

They couldn't believe their fortune when he actually married Anne.

When I eventually dared to open my heart again, after the death of my first husband, who I had married out of duty at a young age, and married the man I chose, I was banished from Court by my own sister.

But the higher you climb, the harder you fall and that was true of our family, certainly true of Anne, whose life culminated in her head lying a few feet away from her body, blood soaking the straw-strewn scaffold.

I think it's fair to say that I won our lifelong competition, but I do pity her, and although my life now is a merry one, I often wonder if roles were reversed, would her fate have been mine?

Helen of Troy

Helen of Troy was a figure in Greek mythology who was said to be the most beautiful woman in the world. She is most famous for leaving her husband Menelaos, King of Sparta, to return to Troy with Paris, Prince of Troy, thereby inciting the Trojan War.

'The face that launched a thousand ships'

I don't wish for any number of ships to be launched for my face.

Is my appearance really the only noteworthy thing about me?

Surely there are many aspects of a person that would make them far worthier of admiration than simply being lucky enough to have been born with pleasing features.

Of course, we all wish for beauty and to be complimented on our appearance can be pleasant, but I wish we weren't reduced to it.

What happens when I am no longer young? Beauty fades.

If my only admirable trait is a pretty face, then what will happen to me when my skin wrinkles and sags, my hair turns grey and I lose the rosy glow in my cheeks and lips? I will fade with my beauty, perhaps I will disappear altogether.

So please, don't just tell me I am beautiful. Try to look deeper. Tell me I'm kind. Tell me I'm clever. Tell me I'm brave.

Anne Hathaway

Anne Hathaway was the wife of William Shakespeare, but knowledge about her is limited. My imagination has therefore run wild on this one.

Think of an iconic Shakespeare line. Go on, any line.

Now what if I told you there's probably a fifty percent chance that I came up with it.

But of course, you could never have known that. Every play, every sonnet was written under the name William Shakespeare.

He would tell me that it did not matter if the people were unaware that it was I who had written what they were hearing or who had created the image they saw, like a man perusing a skull he held in his hand, because he would know and I would know.

He said that was what was important.

I understand, no one would have seen a play with a woman credited as one of the writers, no matter how unjust that seems, but that doesn't mean it hurt any less to hear my husband praised and congratulated on his turn of phrase or genius composition in his latest piece, when it was I who had produced it.

I wrote frequently, sending him ideas and pieces when he was away, but I loved most when he was home and would sit at the table with his quill and parchment, ideas flowing between us both, whilst I busied myself at the hearth, returning often to read over his shoulder.

I recall how my voice used to rise in pitch with my joy when our ideas began to come together and how even his eyes seemed to smile.

Those times will never be forgotten by me, for they were bliss and though I wished for recognition for my work, my life was a relatively content one.

That was before Death visited our household and took our little boy away with him.

Writing became my escape, and I think it did for my husband too, but you see people grieve in different ways and whilst I would have chosen for us to do this together, he preferred to be away in London, alone.

I still send him my writing, but on the occasions few and far between that he does come home, he no longer chooses to write together. His eyes no longer smile and I no longer dance around the table in delight.

Joy has faded from my life, a world once so full of life and colour, now faded to grey.

I wish I could tell you that I don't blame him. But I do.

Pandora

Pandora was a figure from Greek mythology, thought to be the first woman on Earth. Zeus gifted her an elaborately decorated box, forbidding her from ever opening it. However, she did, only to discover that it contained all evils, which she had now released into the world. The only good within the box was hope, which had now also been released.

All I did was open a box.

Yes, I grant you, I was explicitly forbidden from opening it, but it would have been nice if they had told me why.

They say curiosity killed the cat, but quite frankly, I think the cat got a better deal than I did here. The cat may have met its end, but I made one little mistake and took the blame for the misery of humanity for all time.

I'm open to other perspectives, but personally, I think this feels a little out of proportion.

Oh, I almost forgot, my consolation prize: people now have hope.

Like that makes everything better. Now we're just delusional about all the things we have to be miserable about.

Lady Macbeth

Lady Macbeth is the wife of the lead character in Shakespeare's play 'Macbeth'. After he receives a prophecy from three witches that he will be King, Lady Macbeth persuades her husband to kill the existing King, Duncan. With her help, Macbeth succeeds but then gradually distances himself from her. She descends into madness, wracked with guilt, eventually committing suicide.

You think that I do not know that what we did, what I did, was despicable? Well, I do, I recognise my guilt and am surely reaping the consequences of my actions.

I had to call on the powers of darkness to fill me with cruelty. Does that tell you nothing? If I were naturally cruel, I would not have had to ask this.

But if only it had worked, if only I was remorseless.

I could not do it myself, sentiment got in the way and my part in the atrocities that followed has reduced me to this shell of who I was.

I did it for him, for Macbeth, and for what I thought we would build together.

But instead, I unleashed a tyrant, and I no longer recognise the man I married. He used to share with me each plan, each thought, each fear. Now I hear of his brutalities from servants' whispers.

They say I'm mad, but I'm not so sure. I think I simply see through the facade to what we all attempt to conceal: our guilt.

I see crimson coating my hands.

I squeeze my eyes shut: Duncan's wide, expressionless eyes fill my mind.

I open again: maroon congealed under my nails.

Shut: my husband with two daggers dripping in ruby.

I need it to stop, I need this torment to end, but I have only one option.

Wendy

Wendy Darling is a character in the play 'Peter Pan' and the novel 'Peter and Wendy' by J. M. Barry. Peter Pan is a boy who can never grow up and lives on the island of Neverland. He visits the Darlings' house at night and one day, when trying to retrieve his lost shadow, he invites Wendy to join him in Neverland. They have various adventures in Neverland with the Lost Boys, Tinker Bell and Captain Hook, but Wendy and her brothers eventually return home. Peter promises he will come back and take Wendy to Neverland every spring.

Last night I thought I saw your shadow at my window, but when I threw it open, I was met only by the cool night breeze tossing leaves in the street.

The night before I could have sworn I heard your youthful chuckle in the quiet of the dark, but when I swiftly hit the light switch beside my bed, I was met by a still and empty room.

Tonight I think I hear you call my name, a whispered pledge in the unlit room.

But this time I won't reach for the light switch, I will instead try to cling to the fading feeling of your presence for a while longer.

It is always this time, when the light outside is quickly dwindling, that these memories of you surface, and I think I feel you near once again.

Each night for years I would sit at my window, a little light beside me, while I studied the skyline.

But three nights ago, for the first time since we met, I closed my window and I left no light.

Moving on may be a slow process, but I have finished waiting for you.

Some of us do not have the luxury of never growing up.

Mrs Claus

Mrs Claus is the wife of the famous figure of Santa Claus, however, little of the narrative surrounding him seems to include her.

The jolly old man with a pot-belly that shakes when he laughs and a beard as white as snow, who brings gifts and joy to the children of the world.

That is how my husband is described. How am I described? Well, as his wife, or not at all. To be honest, I'm not even sure that he could describe me.

Nick spends more time with his elves than with me and then when he gets home, he's straight off to see the reindeer. I'm sure he prefers their company to mine. Except for Blitzen, he can't stand that poor reindeer because I'm his favourite. It's a sore point between us.

You wouldn't want all the children to know that, would you, Nick? That you withhold carrots from a reindeer because it prefers your wife to you. That's not very jolly at all, is it?

I've had dinner on the table at 7:30pm every day since the day after we were married, so it is hardly a new routine and yet, for the past few years he's been coming home later and later. Dinner has usually been sat on the table for half an hour by the time he comes to eat it. Dining table conversation often goes something like this:

"How's the cottage pie, Nick?"

Grunt.

"Better than last week?"

Belch.

"Well, that's good then."

Then we usually finish the meal in silence.

I loved him once, honestly I did. I was swept off my feet by his charm and that famous twinkle in his eye.

But as I have since seen, he can turn the charm on and off like the flick of a switch and apparently, having been married for so long, I am no longer worth being charming for. There's no point wasting your charm on a prize you have already won, especially when you no longer view them as a prize at all.

But I bet you never saw this coming, Nick.

I am sick and tired of being your cook, cleaner and PA all rolled into one. It is thankless work, I am your wife, not your servant and, frankly, I have reached the end of my tinsel.

The other day you asked me why there were short white hairs in our bed and I made up some story about Dasher escaping again, and I had found her asleep there.

This is exactly what I mean when I tell you that you're losing it because you should have known immediately that I was lying to you.

Why?

Well, because the reindeer aren't white, are they Nick? So, clearly, it wasn't an escaped reindeer.

It was Peter. Unlike you, he appreciates me.

What do you mean, "Peter who?"

Do I have to spell it out for you Nick?

I am having an affair with the Easter Bunny.
I want a divorce; my lawyers will be in touch and good luck hushing this one up.
My bags are packed and I'm leaving tonight to go and live with Peter.
Blitzen's coming too.
Oh, and just for the record, I hate snow.

Printed in Great Britain
by Amazon